A Pig Called
SHRIMP

First published in Great Britain
by HarperCollins Publishers Ltd in 1992
First published in Picture Lions in 1993
Picture Lions is an imprint of the
Children's Division,
part of HarperCollins Publishers Limited
77-85 Fulham Palace Road, Hammersmith,
London W6 8JB

Printed in Great Britain by BPCC Paulton Books

This book is set in 17/24 New Baskerville

A Pig Called SHRIMP

LISA TAYLOR

Illustrated by JONATHAN LANGLEY

PictureLions

An Imprint of HarperCollinsPublishers

Gabriel was a ram. A fine white ram with curling chocolate-coloured horns. And he had a coat which shone like an angel's.

Gabriel was very proud of his bright white coat. Every morning he would roll in the dew to keep it clean. And every afternoon he would walk very slowly round the gorse bush. First one way, then the other, while the thorns tugged at his coat and gently removed all the tangles. The rest of the time Gabriel spent lazing on the banks of the river, chewing grass and gazing at his reflection in the water.

Gabriel didn't have any friends. The only animal he ever
spoke to was a pig who lived on the farm. The pig was
small and pink and liked swimming. Everybody called
him Shrimp.

Every day Shrimp would trot down to the river for a swim.

"Hello, Gabriel!" he would call out. "You look very fine today!"

"Hello!" Gabriel would reply, rather grandly. "Do you think you could swim a bit further down? The ripples will spoil my reflection." Then Shrimp would nod and trot off down the bank.

Shrimp admired Gabriel. He was so huge and
magnificent. Shrimp gazed sadly at his own reflection.
He looked rather as if he had been peeled, he was so
small and pink. How fine to have a coat like candyfloss
snow and two twirling horns instead of bristles!

"I wish I looked like you!" he would say, over and over
again. And Gabriel would nod very wisely and talk at
great length about himself, while Shrimp sat and listened
in wonder.

One day, when Shrimp was swimming out of the way of Gabriel's reflection, he heard Gabriel call him from further up the bank. Shrimp hauled himself out of the water and trotted over.

"There's something floating out there on the river," said Gabriel. "I'd like you to fetch it so I can see what it is." Shrimp screwed up his eyes.

"It's very far out," he said, rather nervously. "And I'm not supposed to stay in the water too long. I'm so small, you see. I might catch cold."

Gabriel stared his haughtiest stare. "Very well," he said and turned away.

"I didn't mean to upset you," Shrimp began hurriedly.
"And it's probably not as far as it looks. Of course I'll go!
Only..." He stopped and snuffled in embarrassment.
"Do you think this means we could be friends!"

Gabriel paused then smiled importantly.

"Certainly," he said. "If it makes you happy." And
squealing with delight, Shrimp plunged into the river.

Gabriel watched from the bank as Shrimp paddled
furiously out across the water. And it wasn't until he was
a tiny pink speck in the distance, that Shrimp turned
and started to paddle back. He was going much slower
now and his head was only just above the water. Gabriel
was rather relieved when he reached the bank. Shrimp
clambered out and dropped the object on the grass.

"It's only an old stick!" he gasped. Then he collapsed,
exhausted, on the ground.

The next day Shrimp didn't
come to swim in the river.
Instead he sent a little bird
with a message:

"Shrimp said to tell his friend
Gabriel that he won't be coming today,"
chirped the little bird. "He's got a cold."

"Oh!" said Gabriel. "I wonder how?"

"I expect it's too much swimming in the river," replied
the little bird, eyeing Gabriel closely.

"Oh well," said Gabriel. "I'm sure he'll get better
soon," and with that he sent the little bird away.

All day long, Gabriel gazed at his reflection while his
coat shone like a halo in the sunlight.

"I wish Shrimp was here to admire it," he thought.

The next morning the little bird came again.

"Shrimp won't be coming today. He said to say he was sorry. And he hopes you'll still be his friend. Only he's feeling a little worse than before."

Gabriel tutted impatiently. "When will he be coming?" he snapped.

"Why don't you ask him?" the little bird chirped. But Gabriel didn't want to leave the river.

Another two days passed and still Shrimp didn't appear.
Gabriel was rather surprised to find that he actually
began to miss him.

It wasn't so much fun looking beautiful when there was
nobody there to admire him. So when, the following
day, the little bird failed to bring a message, Gabriel
decided to go and see Shrimp for himself.

Gabriel walked proudly across the field and up a muddy track to the farm. He half expected somebody to come and meet him. But nobody paid any attention. Nobody except the hens, who clucked and tutted as he passed and the geese, who cackled and hissed.

Gabriel hurried over to where a group of animals stood
huddled around a pen. He could just see the little bird,
perched on one of the bars.

"I've come to see Shrimp!" announced Gabriel, in his
most important voice. But the animals didn't answer.

At last the little bird spoke.

"He's in here!" she said, nodding towards the pen.
And the animals moved aside.

Gabriel didn't recognise Shrimp at first. It wasn't just because he was lying down and covered with straw. It wasn't even because his eyes were closed. It was something else. Something about his colour, which usually glowed so bright and healthy and now looked like a rose which had lost its bloom.

Suddenly Shrimp opened his eyes.

"Gabriel!" he squeaked. "I knew you'd come." And
Gabriel blinked and smiled weakly.

"What's wrong with him?" he asked.

"We don't know," replied the little bird. "He just keeps
shivering. We can't seem to keep him warm," and she turned
sadly back towards the pen. Gabriel hung his head and
walked away.

Gabriel stood on the bank of the river and watched a
huge dark cloud hurry across the sky. He stared at his
reflection in the water. Out of the sunlight, his coat lost
all its sheen and looked horribly dull and dirty. All of a
sudden, Gabriel had an idea.

He galloped up the bank and across the field to where the gorse bush stood on the edge. Then lowering his head, he charged right into the middle. The thorns tore at his coat and pulled it out in great white clumps. Gabriel winced with pain. Then he turned and charged again.

In the field the animals gathered to watch. Overhead
the birds wheeled and cried out in surprise.

   "Gabriel's gone mad! Gabriel's gone mad!"
But Gabriel simply charged on and on, until the bush
was covered with soft white wool.

"Quick!" he called to the birds. "Take it to Shrimp!"

But the birds simply cawed and cried over and over, "Gabriel's gone mad! Gabriel's gone mad!"

"It's to keep Shrimp warm!" screamed Gabriel in desperation. And suddenly the birds understood. Then one by one they swooped from the sky and taking a piece of the coat in their beaks, they soared high above the field to the farm.

Gabriel stood and watched them go. He looked surprisingly small without his fine white coat.

Gabriel visited Shrimp every day after that. And with the help of Gabriel's coat to keep him warm, Shrimp gradually began to recover. But it was a long time before Shrimp was allowed to go swimming again.

Gabriel didn't go to the river anymore. His coat was so thin and uneven now he couldn't bear the sight of his reflection. It didn't matter to Shrimp that Gabriel's coat no longer shimmered in the sunlight. It didn't matter that his horns were scratched and there was a small pink scar above his eye. Shrimp still thought Gabriel was beautiful. But somehow, it was more on the inside now.